Nine Men Chase a Hen

Written by
Barbara Gregorich

Illustrated by
John Sandford

One hen wants a hat.

Two men laugh at that.

Three men have a pet.

Four hens get very wet.

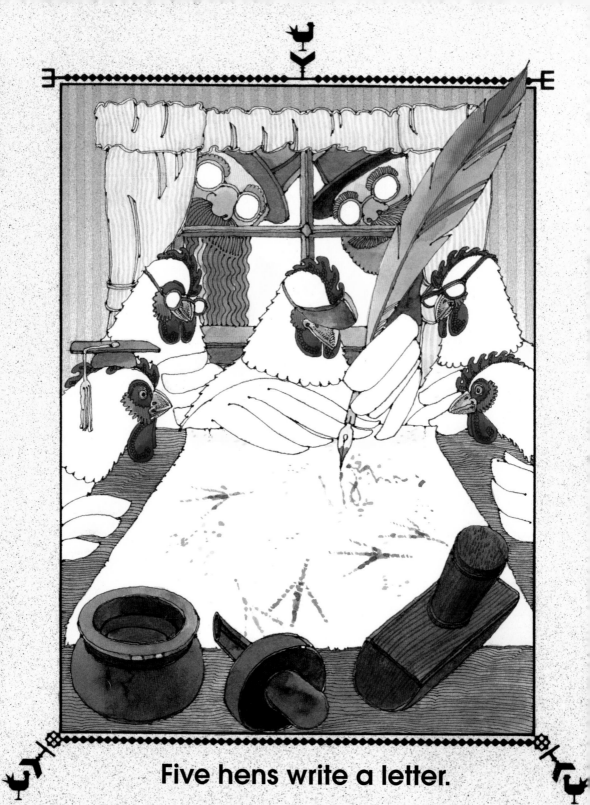

Five hens write a letter.

Six men say theirs is better.

Seven men sleep at night.

Eight hens make it light.

9

Nine men chase a hen.

Ten hens chase the men.

All the men run away.

All the hens begin to play.

Now this funny story ends.

All the men and hens are friends.